Stuck
in the
Muck

Brett Avison · Craig Smith

The Five Mile Press

The Five Mile Press
1 Centre Road, Scoresby, Victoria 3179, Australia
www.fivemile.com.au

Text copyright © Brett Avison, 2011
Illustrations copyright © Craig Smith, 2011
ISBN 9781743002049 (pbk)
First published 2011
Printed in China 5 4 3 2

On Mum and Ted's farm there's a very **large barn**, where the hay and the horses are kept.

And right at the back, past some

seeds in a sack, is where Milky the cow often slept.

This cow was a pet
who hated the wet.
She was happy inside chewing cud.

No-one could explain
why she went in the rain —
and got herself stuck in the mud.

Mum rushed the quad
to the rain-sodden sod,
to drag Milky out of the mud.

But the grass was too slick —
the **wheels** wouldn't stick
to pull Milky out of the mud!

With a **rev** and a **hiccup**,
Ted started the pick-up,
it gave a roar . . . and a thud!

The old engine was tired,
it **misfired** and **expired,**
next to Milky,
still stuck in the mud.

Let's get the truck,
and with some luck,
it won't be such a dud . . .

But now the truck is stuck
in that **black oozy** muck —
and Milky's still there . . . in the mud.

Mum phoned Ken for his bully
with the big metal **pulley**,
to get Milky out of the mud.

The pulley didn't work —
it snapped with a jerk.
Where's Milky? Still stuck in the mud.

'Won't work I'm afraid,
call the fire brigade
to drag Milky out of the mud.'

After a slippery slide

the fire truck's on its side . . .
and Milky is still in the mud.

It was starting to rain,
when they brought in the crane
to lift Milky out of the mud.

With so much broken gear
the crane couldn't get near.
Poor Milky — still stuck in the mud.

There's an airport quite near,
get a chopper out here,
to **lift** this cow out of the mud.

But the noise of the flight
gave our Milky a fright.
Her poor heart started to thud.

Her tail started **thrashing.**
Her legs began lashing —
she jumped right out of the mud!

It took a week and a day
to take the machines all away —
Milky watched while **chewing** her **cud.**

And while she's still a pet
who hates to get wet,
she's Milky no more —
her name's **Mud!**

Also available

A **Bigger Digger**

Right there in the backyard Oscar and Bryn
struck something hard. What they discover as they dig deeper
will surprise everyone. Join these little adventurers and a
whole parade of diggers as they uncover a VERY BIG FIND.